S.

JU

Dave and the Tooth Fairy

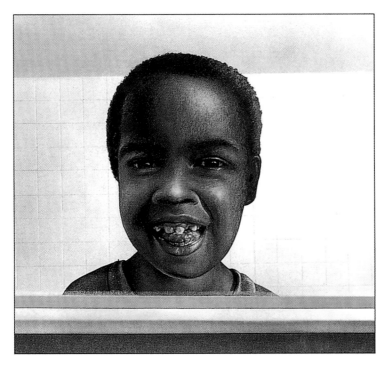

Written by Verna Allette Wilkins • Illustrated by Paul Hunt

Thank you to Renée and Chinwe

For a free color catalog describing Gareth Stevens' list of high-quality books and multimedia programs, call 1-800-542-2595 (USA) or 1-800-461-9120 (Canada). Gareth Stevens Publishing's Fax: (414) 225-0377. See our catalog, too, on the World Wide Web: http://gsinc.com

Library of Congress Cataloging-in-Publication Data

Wilkins, Verna.
   Dave and the tooth fairy / by Verna Allette Wilkins; illustrated by Paul Hunt. — North American ed.
     p. cm.
   Summary: Dave sneezes out his wobbly tooth and then he can't find it, but his grandfather and the tooth fairy get a big surprise when they look under his pillow that night.
   ISBN 0-8368-2089-4 (lib. bdg.)
   [1. Tooth Fairy—Fiction. 2. Teeth—Fiction. 3. Grandfathers—Fiction. 4. African-Americans—Fiction.] I. Hunt, Paul, ill. II. Title
PZ7.W6488Dav 1998
[E]—dc21   97-41908

This U.S. edition first published in 1998 by
Gareth Stevens Publishing
1555 North RiverCenter Drive, Suite 201
Milwaukee, Wisconsin 53212 USA

Original © 1993 Tamarind. This edition of *Dave and the Tooth Fairy*, first published in the United Kingdom in 1993, is published by arrangement with Tamarind, UK.

Printed in the United States of America

1 2 3 4 5 6 7 8 9 02 01 00 99 98

Gareth Stevens Publishing
MILWAUKEE

David Alexander Curtis
had a wobbly tooth.
A very wobbly tooth.

He wibbled it and wobbled it
backward and forward,
but it wouldn't come out.

One day after breakfast, Dave sneezed.
It was his biggest sneeze ever.
His tooth shot out of his mouth,
flew across the room, and disappeared.

3

Dave searched everywhere for his missing tooth.

He looked high and low.
He looked under the table and under the chairs.
No tooth.

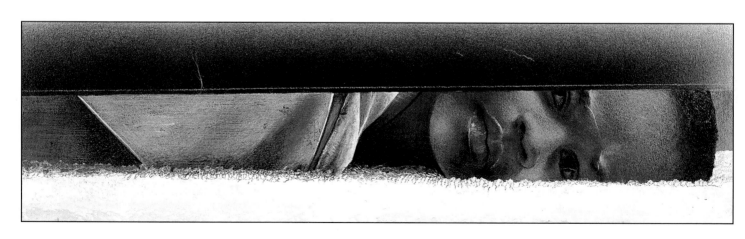

He looked down the side of the old sofa
where everything went.
He found crusty crumbs,
his favorite car, an enormous comb,
and three old buttons —
but no tooth.

No tooth meant no visit from the Tooth Fairy.
No visit from the Tooth Fairy meant no money.
No money meant no kite.
Dave wanted a new kite very much.

5

On the way to school, Dave met his friend Zizwe.

"Do you believe in Tooth Fairies, Ziz?" asked Dave.

"Yes!" Ziz grinned.
"The Tooth Fairy's been to my house four times."

Dave was determined to find his tooth.
But he couldn't.

Then Grandad came to stay.
"I sneezed and lost my tooth, Grandad," said Dave.

"Once, I sneezed so hard all my teeth flew out," Grandad laughed.

"Did you find them?" asked Dave.
"Oh yes. They didn't get very far.
Maybe we'll find yours," said Grandad.

That night, Dave had an excellent idea.
When everyone was fast asleep,
he tiptoed downstairs.
Grandad was asleep on the sofa.

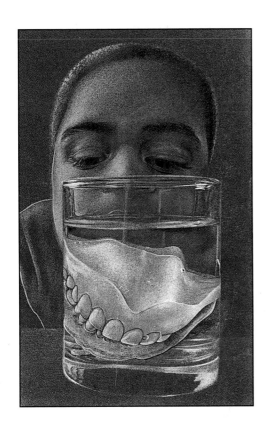

In a strip of light
near the sofa,
on a table, in a glass,
a complete set of teeth
smiled at Dave.

He picked up the glass
and tiptoed back upstairs.

He put the teeth under his
pillow, got back into bed,
and immediately fell fast asleep.

Far, far away in Tooth Fairyland, Afiya sat alone on duty.
She had been a Tooth Fairy for a long time.
Afiya liked her work, but she longed for a job
where she could meet children in the daytime when they were awake.

Then Dave's tooth call came.
Afiya quickly prepared herself for her journey.
She spread her bright wings
and flew into the night toward Dave's house.

It was a clear, warm night.
She heard the hoot
of an owl far away,
and a bat came close
as she flew.

At last, by the light of the moon, she floated into Dave's room.

One tooth,
Two teeth . . .
Thirty-two teeth!
I can't afford all these!

Back she flew,
over trees,
over hills,
over clouds,
to Tooth Fairyland.
It was her fastest
flight ever.

In Dave's house,
Grandad yawned and got up.
He stepped on something sharp.
"Ouch! It's Dave's tooth,"
he whispered.

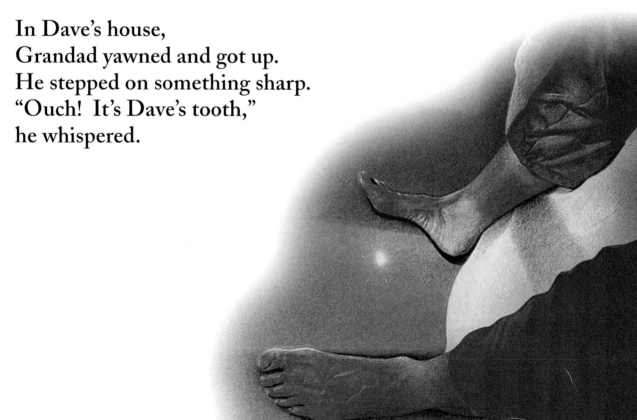

Grandad crept upstairs.
Very quietly and very gently,
he lifted Dave's pillow.

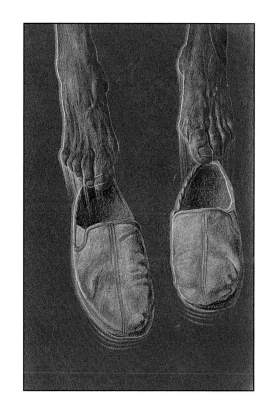

He nearly jumped
right out of his slippers!
His own teeth were smiling at him.
He did a swap.
It was his quickest swap ever.

Just before the sun peeped over the hills,
a very tired Tooth Fairy flew
back into Dave's room.

Under his pillow, she found just one little tooth
that looked exactly like a crusty crumb.

"Where have all those teeth gone?" she wondered.

It was nearly daylight,
so Afiya quickly collected the single tooth
and put some money under Dave's pillow.
Then, with a flash of bright wings,
she set off once again for Tooth Fairyland.

When she arrived back in her office,
Afiya found a letter on her desk.

She had a new job. Good news, great news!
Her best news ever!
Afiya was delighted.
In her new job, she would meet lots of children in the daytime.

At 8 o'clock exactly, David Alexander Curtis jumped out of bed and looked under his pillow. He ran downstairs to see Grandad.

Dave was delighted.
He had enough money to buy his kite.
Grandad had his teeth.
Afiya was manager of the kite shop,
where loads of kids went shopping.

23

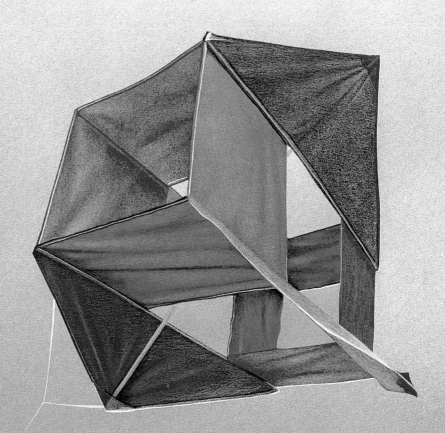

Near his house,
on a hill,
in a field,
David Alexander Curtis flew his kite —
his biggest kite ever.